TALL AND SMALL

All inquiries should be addressed to:
Barron's Educational Series, Inc.
250 Wireless Boulevard
Hauppauge, NY 11788

International Standard Book Number 0-8120-1840-0

Library of Congress Catalog Card Number 93-32337

Library of Congress Cataloging-In-Publication Data

Foster, Kelli C.
    Tall and small / by Foster & Erickson ; illustrations by Kerri
Gifford.
        p.   cm. —(Get ready—get set—read!)
    Summary: A horse named Stonewall loves to play ball against the wall
belonging to a pack rat named Snowball.
    ISBN 0-8120-1840-0
    (1. Animals—Fiction. 2. Stories in rhyme.) I. Erickson, Gina Clegg.
II. Gifford, Kerri, ill. III. Title. IV. Series: Erickson, Gina Clegg.
Get ready—get set—read!
PZ8.3.F813Tal   1994
(E)—dc20   93-32337
                                                                                CIP
                                                                                AC

PRINTED IN HONG KONG
12 11 10 9 8

GET READY...GET SET...READ!

TALL AND SMALL

by
Foster & Erickson

Illustrations by
Kerri Gifford

BARRON'S

In a barn, in a stall,

ved Stonewall and Snowball.

"I am called Stonewall.
I play ball."

"All day long I hit this wall."
Bam!

Bam!
"I'm called Snowball."

"I find and keep things
in this wall."
Bam!

"I wish Stonewall would not
play ball on my wall."
Bam!

"All my things fall
when his ball hits my wall."

"My ball went into the hall.
I cannot get it, I'm too tall."

Look! There is Stonewall's ball.
will keep it in my wall."

"Snowball can help me,
she is small. Oh Snowball…"

"Stonewall is calling.
Should I give him the ball?
If I do, he'll hit my wall."

"Oh Snowball,
have you seen my ball?"

"Yes I found it in the hall.
But will you play
on the other wall?"

Now in a barn, in a stall,
all is well with
Stonewall and Snowball.

The End

The ALL Word Family

all
ball
called
calling
fall
hall
small
Snowball
stall
Stonewall
tall
wall

Sight Words

day
now
barn
give
he'll
play
found
other
would
should
things

Dear Parents and Educators:

Welcome to **Get Ready...Get Set...Read!**

We've created these books to introduce children to the magic of reading.

Each story in the series is built around one or two word families. For example, *A Mop for Pop* uses the OP word family. Letters and letter blends are added to OP to form words such as TOP, LOP, and STOP. As you can see, once children are able to read OP, it is a simple task for them to read the entire word family. In addition to word families, we have used a limited number of "sight words." These are words found to occur with high frequency in books your child will soon be reading. Being able to identify sight words greatly increases reading skill.

You might find the steps outlined on the facing page useful in guiding your work with your beginning reader.

We had great fun creating these books, and great pleasure sharing them with our children. We hope *Get Ready...Get Set...Read!* helps make this first step in reading fun for you and your new reader.

Kelli C. Foster, PhD
Educational Psychologist

Gina Clegg Erickson, MA
Reading Specialist

Guidelines for Using *Get Ready...Get Set...Read!*

Step 1.   Read the story to your child.

Step 2.   Have your child read the Word Family list aloud several times.

Step 3.   Invent new words for the list. Print each new combination for your child to read. Remember, nonsense words can be used (*dat, kat, gat*).

Step 4.   Read the story *with* your child. He or she reads all of the Word Family words; you read the rest.

Step 5.   Have your child read the Sight Word list aloud several times.

Step 6.   Read the story *with* your child again. This time he or she reads the words from both lists; you read the rest.

Step 7.   Your child reads the entire book to you!

There are five sets of books in the

Series. Each set consists of five **FIRST BOOKS** and two **BRING-IT-ALL-TOGETHER BOOKS**.

SET 1

is the first set your children should read.
The word families are selected from the short vowel sounds:
at, **ed**, **ish** and **im**, **op**, **ug**.

SET 2

provides more practice
with short vowel sounds:
an and **and**, **et**, **ip**, **og**, **ub**.

SET 3

focuses on
long vowel sounds:
ake, **eep**, **ide** and **ine**, **oke** and **ose**, **ue** and **ute**.

SET 4

introduces the idea that the word family sounds
can be spelled two different ways:
ale/ail, **een/ean**, **ight/ite**, **ote/oat**, **oon/une**.

SET 5

acquaints children with word families that
do not follow the rules for long and short vowel sounds:
all, **ound**, **y**, **ow**, **ew**.